THE GRAPHIC NOVI

GREAT
EXPECTATIONS

Published by
Evans Brothers Limited
2A Portman Mansions
Chiltern Street
London W1U 6NR

Reprinted 2009

British Library Cataloguing in Publication Data
Burningham, Hilary
Great Expectations – Graphic novels
1. England – Social conditions – 19th century – Juvenile fiction
2. Bildungsromane
3. Children's stories
I. Title II. Dickens, Charles, 1812-1870
823.9'14[J]

ISBN 978 0 237 52315 2

Printed in Dubai

THE GRAPHIC NOVELS SERIES

GREAT EXPECTATIONS

CHARLES DICKENS

RETOLD BY HILARY BURNINGHAM
ILLUSTRATED BY TRACY FENNELL

EVANS BROTHERS LIMITED

Volume One

My name is Pip – short for Philip. I live in a village with my sister and her husband, Mr Joe Gargery, the village blacksmith. I live with my sister because my parents and my five little brothers are dead. They are all buried in the churchyard nearby.

One day I was in the churchyard, near their graves, when a frightening man grabbed me. He had a great iron on his leg and a dirty old rag tied round his head. He threatened to cut my throat.

I had some bread in my pocket, which he ate hungrily. He made me promise to meet him early the next morning. I was to take him a file and some food, and meet him at a place called The Battery[1]. If not, terrible things would happen to me.

He had a friend, he said, a young man, even more frightening than himself who would cut out my heart and liver if I didn't do as he said.

I was terrified. I ran all the way home without stopping.

---

[1] Battery – old defence workings, such as gun emplacements

'You fail or you go from my words in any partickler, no matter how small it is, and your heart and your liver shall be tore out, roasted and ate.'

I got home late and my sister hit me with her stick.
When I was given my bread for supper, I slipped it
down the leg of my trousers. It was Christmas Eve.
I took my turn stirring the Christmas pudding.

In the distance, we heard a great gun going off. Joe
said a convict had escaped, perhaps two. I was
helping an escaped convict! But I had to do what
I had promised.

Early the next morning, I stole some more bread,
some cheese, a meat bone, half a jar of mincemeat,
a pork pie and some brandy. I filled the brandy
bottle with tar water[1] so that no one would notice.
Last, I took a file from where Joe kept his tools.

On the way to The Battery I met another man.
I thought he was the friend my convict had spoken
about. He tried to hit me and ran away.

I went to The Battery and there was the right man.
Shivering with cold, he drank the brandy and ate
the food. When I told him about the other man, he
became worried. I left him filing off his leg-iron,
determined to catch the other man.

[1] tar water – a very nasty-tasting medicine, the same colour as brandy

He swallowed, or rather snapped up every mouthful too soon and too fast; and he looked sideways here and there while he ate, as if he thought there was danger in every direction, of somebody's coming to take the pie away.

On Christmas Day, we had our usual visitors:
Mr Wopsle, Mr and Mrs Hubble, and 'Uncle'
Pumblechook.

Mr Wopsle had a deep voice he was very proud of,
while Mr Pumblechook always enjoyed telling me
how fortunate I was. Mr Pumblechook became
thirsty, and my sister offered him some brandy.
I remembered the tar water! Mr Pumblechook took
a great gulp of the brandy and almost choked.
Fortunately, no one thought of suspecting me.

Next, my sister asked if anyone would like to have
some pork pie. It had been a present from Mr
Pumblechook, and I knew it was no longer in the
larder[1] – I had stolen it that morning. Now I would
certainly be found out.

Just as she went to find it, a group of soldiers
arrived at the front door. They were looking for two
convicts on the marshes. Everyone forgot about the
pork pie.

[1] larder – large, cool cupboard for keeping food, usually next to the kitchen

Instantly afterwards, the company were seized with unspeakable consternation, owing to his springing to his feet, turning round several times in an appalling spasmodic whooping-cough dance, and rushing out at the door.

The soldiers had come to get a set of handcuffs repaired. Mrs Joe, my sister, offered them all drinks. They stood around in the forge, watching Joe get his fire going. Mr Pumblechook got quite merry and kept filling up their glasses.

I couldn't help thinking about the convicts out on the marshes.

When the handcuffs were repaired, the soldiers left to look for the convicts. Mr Wopsle, Joe and I followed them to see what happened.

They found the convicts fighting in a ditch. My convict said that he had taken the other one prisoner. He had got rid of his leg-iron and could have got away, but he wanted to catch the other man and send him back to prison. My convict also said that he had stolen food from our house, including the pork pie. At least now I wouldn't get into trouble over the missing food.

We watched the soldiers take away both men and then we went home. I was so tired that Joe carried me on his shoulders.

'I took him! I give him up to you! Mind that!'
'It's not much to be particular about,' said the sergeant; 'it'll do
you small good, my man, being in the same plight yourself.
Handcuffs there!'

Then a strange thing happened. I was invited to the house of Miss Havisham, to go and play there. Everyone in the village knew Miss Havisham. She was supposed to be very rich, and lived in a big, gloomy old house. Mr Pumblechook paid his rent to her, and he had given her my name.

When I went to the house I was met by a girl of about the same age as myself. She was very beautiful, but cold and unfriendly. She called me *Boy*. She told me the name of the house was Satis House. *Satis* meant *enough* in Greek.

The girl, Estella, took me in to Miss Havisham. Miss Havisham was a very old lady, dressed like a bride. She had beautiful clothes, jewels and lovely furniture, but everything was old and covered in dust. All the clocks had stopped at twenty-to-nine. She told me that she had a broken heart.

Miss Havisham watched Estella and me play cards. We played *Beggar My Neighbour*. Estella made fun of me. She said I was a stupid, clumsy working boy. She also said I was common. *And* she beat me at cards!

'He calls the knaves, Jacks, this boy!' said Estella with disdain before our first game was out. 'And what coarse hands he has. And what thick boots!'

When I got home, my sister wanted to know all about the big house. Mr Pumblechook came for a visit because he wanted to know, too.

I somehow felt it was wrong to gossip about Miss Havisham, so I made up the details instead. I told them that she was tall and dark. I said that she sat in a black velvet coach and that, with Estella, we had cake and wine on gold plates. I said that she had four huge dogs that fought over meat brought to them in a silver basket.

They believed every word I said. It was all lies, and I didn't care until Joe came in. Joe had always been so kind to me, I couldn't bear to lie to him.

When we were alone, I told him the truth. Dear Joe said that, no matter what, it was wrong to tell lies and I must never do it again.

'There's one thing you may be sure of, Pip,' said Joe, after some rumination, 'namely, that lies is lies. Howsever they come, they didn't ought to come, and they come from the father of lies, and work round to the same. Don't you tell no more of 'em, Pip. That ain't the way to get out of being common, old chap.'

Now that I had met Estella and Miss Havisham,
I didn't want them to think me common any more.
I decided to learn as much as I could from Mr
Wopsle's great-aunt and her granddaughter, Biddy.

I went to 'school' with them in the evenings, but
they weren't proper teachers and none of the pupils
learned very much.

On my way home, I used to call for Joe at our
village pub, the Three Jolly Bargemen. One night,
a stranger bought Joe a drink. He asked a lot of
questions about the village, and stared at me very
hard. He stirred his drink with a file: Joe's file. I was
the only one who saw it. He had the file; he knew
the convict I had helped.

As Joe and I left, the man gave me a shilling[1]
wrapped up in some paper. When we got home, we
discovered that he had wrapped the shilling in two
one-pound notes[2]. He must have made a mistake.
My sister put the pound notes in a teapot on the
shelf. We would have to give them back when he
found out.

---

[1] shilling – silver coin, similar to a modern 10p coin, worth about 5p
[2] one-pound notes – replaced by the one-pound coin in 1983

I knew it to be Joe's file, and I knew that he knew my convict, the moment I saw the instrument.

The next time I went to Miss Havisham's, she had several visitors – Miss Sarah Pocket, Mr and Mrs Raymond Pocket (her name was Camilla), and a very serious lady named Georgiana. I also met a large man on the stairs, who told me to behave myself. I had no idea then that he would one day be very important in my life.

It was Miss Havisham's birthday, but no one was allowed to mention it. She walked with me, resting her hand on my shoulder. This time we were in a different room. It had a large dining table, all set out for a feast with a huge, old, crumbling wedding cake in the middle of it. Estella and the Pockets came in and watched us. I felt embarrassed.

Afterwards, I met another visitor, a boy my own age with a pale face. He wanted a fight, so I fought him. I beat him easily, giving him a black eye. Estella may have seen the fight. When she let me out she was flushed and excited. She let me kiss her.

It was late when I got home. What a long, strange day.

The second greatest surprise I have ever had in my life was seeing him on his back again, looking up at me out of a black eye.

I didn't see the pale young man again at Miss Havisham's. Mostly, I would push her in a garden-chair[1] around her dressing room and the dining-room. She would often ask me about Estella. 'Does she grow prettier and prettier?' she would say.

Mr Pumblechook and my sister thought that Miss Havisham planned to help me one day. Joe and I had always thought that he would teach me to be a blacksmith. I would become his apprentice[2].

One day, Miss Havisham, seeing that I was growing tall, said that it was time I began my apprenticeship. She said that Joe and I should bring the papers to her. Joe wore his best clothes and was very uncomfortable. Miss Havisham gave Joe twenty-five guineas[3], the money I had earned on my visits. It seemed a lot of money.

Mr Pumblechook took Joe and me to the Town Hall. My papers had to be signed by the justices[4]. That night, I was very unhappy. I no longer wanted to be a blacksmith. I had once, but I felt differently about everything since meeting Estella.

[1] garden chair – a kind of light wicker wheelchair
[2] apprentice – legal agreement between a boy and his employer. The boy worked for no (or very little) money in exchange for training
[3] twenty-five guineas – £26.25p
[4] justices – judges

'Pip has earned a premium here,' she said, 'and here it is. There are five-and-twenty guineas in this bag. Give it to your master, Pip?'

Before I met Miss Havisham and Estella, being Joe's apprentice and learning a trade was just what I wanted. It was not what I wanted any more. I felt ashamed of what I did and where I lived. I didn't want Estella to know.

I didn't tell Joe any of this. He was a good, kind man. I loved him and didn't want to hurt his feelings.

I tried in every way to improve myself. I tried to learn from Mr Wopsle's great-aunt. I tried to learn from Biddy. I even tried to learn from Mr Wopsle, but he liked to act and pretended I was a character in a play, and sometimes he hit me.

Joe and I would go out on the marshes and I would try to teach him what I had learned. Joe didn't remember very much of it, but he smoked his pipe as we chatted together.

One day, a year after I had started my apprenticeship, I asked Joe for a half-day. I wanted to visit Miss Havisham. I said I wanted to thank her for her help. Of course, I was hoping to see Estella, too. Joe agreed.

'Yes, Joe; but what I wanted to say, was, that as we are rather slack just now, if you would give me a half-holiday tomorrow, I think I would go up-town and make a call on Miss Est— Havisham.'

Joe had another helper at the smithy, a man called Orlick. We didn't like each other. When Orlick heard that I was to have an afternoon off, he demanded one, too. Peace-loving Joe said that it would be a half-holiday for everyone.

My sister was listening at the window. She thought it was a waste of money to give everyone a half-day off. She went on the rampage. She screamed at Joe that he was stupid and called Orlick a rogue. Orlick told her that she was a 'foul shrew' and said that if she were his wife, he would hold her under the water pump and choke her.

Joe could not allow Orlick to insult his wife. They fought, and Orlick was soon on the floor in the coal-dust. No one could stand up against Joe; he was the strongest man in our neighbourhood.

Later, the row seemed to be over. Mrs Joe was quiet and Joe and Orlick shared a beer after their fight.

'O! To hear him!' cried my sister, with a clap of her hands and a scream together – which was her next stage. 'To hear the names he's giving me! That Orlick! In my own house! Me, a married woman! With my husband standing by! O! O!'

I went to Miss Havisham's as I had planned. I told her that I was doing well and thanked her for her help. Estella was not there. She had gone abroad. Miss Havisham was delighted to see my disappointment.

I spent the evening reading with Mr Wopsle at Pumblechook's house. As we walked home, we met Orlick.

Although it was late, eleven o'clock, there were a lot of people at the Three Jolly Bargemen. This was quite unusual. Mr Wopsle went to find out what was the matter. He came running out and told me to get home fast. Orlick ran with us.

When we reached the smithy, the yard was full of people and there was a surgeon in the kitchen with Joe. My sister was lying on the floor with a terrible injury to her head.

Near where she lay was a convict's leg-iron, which had been filed off. It had to be the one my convict had filed off on the marshes. That was a long time ago. I was sure that Orlick had struck my sister with the leg-iron, or perhaps it was the strange man who had shown me the file at the Three Jolly Bargemen.

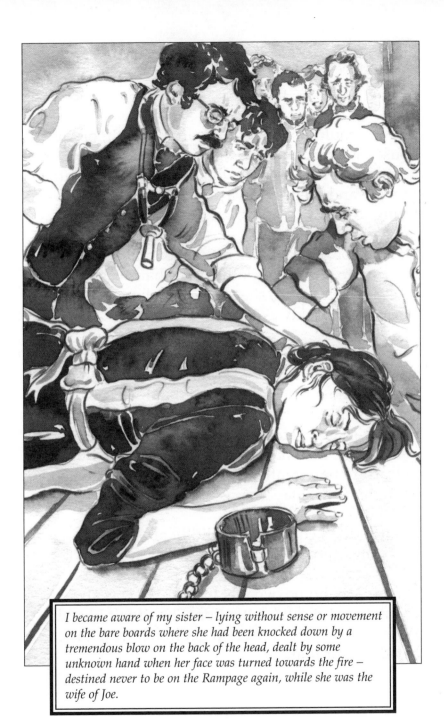

I became aware of my sister – lying without sense or movement on the bare boards where she had been knocked down by a tremendous blow on the back of the head, dealt by some unknown hand when her face was turned towards the fire – destined never to be on the Rampage again, while she was the wife of Joe.

Mrs Joe could no longer look after herself, or the house. She couldn't speak properly. Biddy came to take care of us. She was wonderful at looking after Mrs Joe and seemed always to know what she was trying to say.

Slowly, I began to notice a change in Biddy. She wore more attractive clothes. Her hair was done nicely. When I read, she studied with me, and learned as quickly as I did.

One Sunday afternoon, Biddy and I took a walk together. I told her about Estella: how beautiful she was, and how she had told me that I was coarse and common. Biddy thought those words were rude and untrue. To her, Estella did not sound like a very nice person. She may have been right. Even so, I wanted to learn to be a gentleman so that I would be good enough for Estella.

I found that I could talk to Biddy about anything that came into my head.

On the way home, we met Orlick. He was always trying to get Biddy's attention. She didn't like him. Whenever I could, I tried to get in his way. Orlick hated me for that.

'Well then, understand once for all that I never shall or can be comfortable – or anything but miserable – there, Biddy! – unless I can lead a very different sort of life from the life I lead now.'

One night, a man came to the Three Jolly Bargemen and asked to speak privately to Joe and me. I realised I had met him once before, on the stairs at Miss Havisham's. His name was Mr Jaggers and he was a lawyer. He told us that he was acting for someone else, and that I had 'great expectations'. One day, I would get what he called a 'handsome property'. He asked Joe if he would release me from my apprenticeship, to which Joe replied, 'Of course.'

Mr Jaggers now told me that, because of my new expectations in life, I would need a better education. That was just what I had been longing for. I was to study with a Mr Matthew Pocket. That would mean moving to London. Jaggers gave me twenty guineas to buy new clothes and told me to be ready to travel to London in one week. He offered Joe some money to end the apprenticeship but Joe refused it. He seemed almost angry at the offer.

I had met Mr Jaggers and some members of the Pocket family at Satis House, and I had heard the name of Matthew Pocket there. I was certain that Miss Havisham was behind this change in my fortunes.

'I am instructed to communicate to him,' said Mr Jaggers,
throwing his finger at me, sideways, 'that he will come into
a handsome property. Further [...] that he be immediately
removed from his present sphere of life and from this place, and
be brought up as a gentleman – in a word, as a young fellow of
great expectations.'

Before I left, I spoke with Biddy. I asked her to help Joe improve his manners so that he could fit in better with my new life. Biddy looked at me very strangely when I said this. She asked, 'Won't his manners do, then?' Perhaps she was jealous of my good fortune.

I went into the village and ordered my new clothes from Mr Trabb, the tailor. After I had seen the tailor, Mr Pumblechook gave me lunch. He was very nice to me. He seemed to feel that I owed all my good luck to him.

I went to say goodbye to Miss Havisham. She already knew I was going away. I was more sure than ever that she was paying for my new life.

The night before I left for London, I put on my new clothes for Joe and Biddy. The next morning, I left the forge very early. Suddenly, I realised how much I was going to miss Joe and Biddy, especially Joe. After saying goodbye, I cried as I walked along the road to get the coach for London.

I stopped then, to wave my hat, and dear old Joe waved his strong right arm above his head, crying huskily 'Hooroar!' and Biddy put her apron to her face.

Volume Two

I took the stagecoach[1] to London and a hackney-carriage[2] to Mr Jaggers' office. While I waited for him, I went out for a walk.

First, I saw Smithfield, where the meat market was. It was filthy with grease and the blood of the animals. Next I saw Newgate Prison, and the place where prisoners were hanged and whipped in public. London was supposed to be the best place in the whole world, but many of the things I saw were dirty and evil.

Everyone knew Mr Jaggers, my guardian. He earned his money by arguing cases in court. He was very good at what he did. People seemed frightened of him. He had a lot of power to help people – or not.

Mr Jaggers had arranged for me to stay for a few days at a place called Barnard's Inn with a young Mr Pocket. On Monday we were to go to his father's house. I was to have a good allowance and Jaggers gave me the cards of tradesmen I should deal with. His clerk, Mr Wemmick took me round to Barnard's Inn.

---

[1] stagecoach – large, horse-drawn carriage, carrying a number of passengers and following a regular route
[2] hackney-carriage – a taxi, in those days a small, horse-drawn coach

So imperfect was this realisation of the first of my great expectations, that I looked in dismay at Mr Wemmick.

At first Barnard's Inn did not seem very nice. It was dirty and the stairs and windows were in very bad condition.

When at last young Mr Pocket arrived, I was very surprised. It was the pale young man I had fought and beaten at Miss Havisham's. He even apologised for hurting me! His name was Herbert, and he was to help me improve my manners. He did it in a kind, funny way, which made us both laugh and we got on well together.

Herbert didn't like the name 'Philip', and asked if he could call me 'Handel' instead. Handel was a famous composer who, he said, had written a piece of music called the *Harmonious Blacksmith*. After that, Herbert always called me Handel.

He knew a lot about Miss Havisham and how she came to be so strange. After dinner he told me her sad story.

'Then, my dear Handel,' said he, turning round as the door opened, 'here is the dinner, and I must beg of you to take the top of the table, because the dinner is of your providing.'

Herbert told me that Miss Havisham came from a wealthy family. When her father died she became a rich young woman. She had a half-brother who was lazy and wasted all his money. She fell in love with his friend who, with her half-brother, planned to cheat her out of her money.

Miss Havisham and the friend planned to be married. They fixed their wedding date, the wedding clothes were bought and the guests were invited.

On the day of the wedding, at twenty minutes to nine, Miss Havisham received a letter from her fiancé, calling off the wedding. Before breaking off the wedding, her fiancé and her half-brother had swindled a lot of money out of her. She was left broken-hearted, with most of her money gone.

Twenty minutes to nine! Now I understood why all the clocks at Satis House were stopped at that time.

After that, Miss Havisham adopted Estella. Herbert had no idea who Estella's real parents were. Miss Havisham wanted Estella to grow up and break men's hearts, just as hers had been broken.

'The day came, but not the bridegroom. He wrote her a letter—'
'Which she received,' I struck in, 'when she was dressing for
her marriage? At twenty minutes to nine?'
'At the hour and minute,' said Herbert, nodding, 'at which she
afterwards stopped all the clocks.'

On the Monday we went to the home of Herbert's family. Besides his parents, Mr and Mrs Pocket, Herbert's four younger sisters and two younger brothers, as well as a baby lived there. Everything was quite chaotic!

There were two nursemaids[1], Flopson and Miller, and several other servants. The servants ran the house and sometimes cheated Mr and Mrs Pocket. There were also two other boarders, by the names of Drummle and Startop.

It was a very busy, disorganised house. When it all got too much for Mr Pocket, he would put his hands to his head and try to lift himself up by his hair. It was a very strange gesture, but everyone was used to it and no one took any notice.

After dinner we all went rowing on the river. It was so pleasant that I decided to get myself a rowing boat. I also decided to keep my room at Barnard's Inn with Herbert. I would sometimes need just to be with Herbert, away from the Pockets' house.

---

[1] nursemaids – women paid to look after babies and small children

He laid down the carving-knife and fork – being engaged in carving, at the moment – put his two hands into his disturbed hair, and appeared to make an extraordinary effort to lift himself up by it.

Drummle's full name was Bentley Drummle. As I
got to know him better, I liked him less and less. His
family was rich and he would probably have a title
one day, but he was lazy, stupid, and unpleasant.

Startop and I got on well, and we often chatted as
we rowed on the river.

But Herbert was my best friend and companion.
I gave him a half-share in my boat and we often
walked together from Barnard's Inn to Hammersmith,
where the Pockets lived.

One day, I went to visit Wemmick, Mr Jaggers' clerk,
at his home in Walworth. It was the strangest, and
the smallest, house I had ever seen. He kept a pig
and hens and rabbits, and grew vegetables. He also
looked after his father, whom he called 'Aged parent'.
His father was deaf and we had to shout at him.
Wemmick's small, cosy house seemed very far away
from Jaggers' smart office and Newgate Prison.

There we found, sitting by a fire, a very old man in a flannel coat: clean, cheerful, comfortable, and well cared for, but intensely deaf.
'Well, Aged parent,' said Wemmick, shaking hands with him in a cordial and jocose way, 'how am you?'

Next, I was invited to dine with Mr Jaggers. He also invited Bentley Drummle, Startop and Herbert Pocket. As I have said, I did not like Drummle. He was a heavy, unpleasant man. For some reason, Mr Jaggers called Drummle 'the Spider' and seemed to like him.

Mr Jaggers' housekeeper did the cooking. Wemmick had told me to take particular notice of her. She was a strange woman with long, flowing hair. Jaggers made her show us her wrists, one of which was badly scarred. He said that she had very strong hands. All this seemed very strange and did not make sense to me until much later.

We all had too much to drink and there were silly arguments. I apologised to Mr Jaggers, and he told me again how much he liked Drummle. About a month later, Drummle left the Pockets for good.

'Very few men have the power of wrist that this woman has.
It's remarkable what mere force of grip there is in these hands.'

One morning Joe came to see me at Barnard's Inn
with a message from Miss Havisham. Estella had
come home and wished to see me. Joe also said
that Mr Wopsle had now become an actor. He was
playing in *Hamlet* at a small London theatre. Joe was
very uncomfortable with me now and in these smart
surroundings, so he did not stay long.

The next day, I caught the afternoon stagecoach to
the village. Two convicts were also travelling on the
coach with their keeper. I recognised one of them –
it was the man from the Three Jolly Bargemen who
had given me the two pound notes and the shilling!
I heard him telling the other convict about the
pound notes. They had been given to him by
another convict to give to the 'boy that had fed him
and kep' his secret.' He was talking about me ...

I got off the coach as soon as I could, and went to
the Blue Boar. I told myself that there were all kinds
of good reasons why I should stay at the inn, but in
my heart I knew I should have stayed at the forge
with Joe and Biddy.

'So he says,' resumed the convict I had recognised, 'it was all said and done in half a minute, behind a pile of timber in the Dockyard – "You're going to be discharged?" Yes, I was. Would I find out that boy that had fed him and kep' his secret, and give him them two one-pound notes? Yes, I would. And I did.'

The next day, at Satis House, I got a surprise. Orlick opened the door. It seemed he was working for Miss Havisham. Sarah Pocket was there, too.

When I entered Miss Havisham's dressing-room, she was in her usual place with a beautiful lady I had never seen before. But I *had* seen her before: it was Estella! She had just returned from France and was to come to London. Miss Havisham told us to walk together, which we did. We walked in the overgrown garden. There was something about Estella now that reminded me of someone else, but I couldn't work out who it might be.

Estella tried to warn me that she had no heart, that she could not love. Yet, later, Miss Havisham told me to love her. I was sure that she had chosen us for each other.

Mr Jaggers was there, too. That night we played cards: Jaggers, Miss Havisham, Estella and myself. I had never seen Estella looking so beautiful!

The next morning, I told Mr Jaggers what I knew about Orlick. He agreed that Orlick could not be allowed to stay at Satis House and immediately went to pay him off.

We played until nine o'clock, and then it was arranged that when Estella came to London I should be forewarned of her coming and should meet her at the coach; and then I took leave of her, and touched her and left her.

When I got back to London, I told Herbert that
I loved Estella more than ever. I knew then that
I would always love her.

Herbert, in turn, told me that he was engaged to
be married – but it was a secret. The young lady's
name was Clara. As soon as he was earning some
money they would be married. For now, though,
she looked after her father who was an invalid.

Herbert was quite depressed about his lack of
money. To cheer him up, I suggested that we go
to see Mr Wopsle in Shakespeare's *Hamlet*.

Poor Mr Wopsle! The audience was very rude and
noisy, constantly interrupting him. *Hamlet* is a very
serious play, but they laughed and made jokes all
the way through. Herbert and I felt sorry for him.

When we saw Mr Wopsle afterwards, he didn't
seem to realise how bad the play had been. Herbert
and I told him it had gone very well, and invited
him back to supper.

Whenever that undecided Prince had to ask a question or state a doubt, the public helped him out with it. As for example; on the question whether 'twas nobler in the mind to suffer, some roared yes, and some no, and some inclining to both opinions said, 'toss up for it,' and quite a Debating Society arose.

I received a note from Estella. She was coming to London two days later! I was so excited that I arrived at the coach-office four or five hours too early. As I walked about to pass the time, I met Mr Wemmick on his way to Newgate Prison. Although I didn't want to leave the coach-office for fear of missing Estella, I went with him. Again, I was impressed with Mr Jaggers' power and influence.

At last it was time for Estella to arrive. She was wearing a fur-trimmed travelling dress and looked more beautiful than ever.

We had tea at the inn, then I took Estella to the big house in Richmond where she was to stay. I returned to Mr Matthew Pocket's house at Hammersmith, as it was closer to Richmond than Barnard's Inn.

My heart was aching. When would I see Estella again? And there was something else – I still had the feeling of a mystery unsolved; of Estella reminding me of someone else, someone I had seen recently. But who was it?

The doorway soon absorbed her boxes, and she gave me her hand and a smile, and said goodnight, and was absorbed likewise. And still I stood looking at the house, thinking how happy I should be if I lived there with her, and knowing that I never was happy with her, but always miserable.

At about this time, Herbert and I began to get into debt. Although Herbert was always looking for work, he was still not earning any money. For appearence's sake, I had taken on a manservant whom I called 'the Avenger'. I couldn't really afford the Avenger. He had to have a special uniform, and didn't do very much.

From time to time, Herbert and I would sit down and add up all our bills. We would sort everything into piles and then add up how much we owed. We always felt better after doing this, even though we were spending a lot more than we were getting. In fact, we would often go out and spend some more money and run up more bills!

One night we had just finished sorting out the bills and adding them up when a letter arrived. It had a heavy black border and a black seal[1]. It was from Trabb & Co. in the village. My sister, Mrs Joe Gargery, had passed away. The funeral was the following Monday. Of course, I had to go.

[1] seal – melted wax used to seal an envelope, and stamped with an official badge or emblem

TRABB & CO. [...] begged to inform me that Mrs J. Gargery had departed this life on Monday last, at twenty minutes past six in the evening, and that my attendance was requested at the interment on Monday next at three o'clock in the afternoon.

A funeral in the village was a very solemn, serious affair. Mr Trabb made sure that everyone was properly dressed and behaved as he expected them to.

Everyone was there: Biddy in a simple black dress, Uncle Pumblechook in a black cloak and yards of black hatband, and dear Joe in a small cloak with a huge bow.

Mr Trabb told everyone to put handkerchiefs to their faces as we walked through the village. We looked as if we all had nosebleeds! My sister was laid to rest in the churchyard, not far from my father and my mother.

That night I asked to stay in my own little room, and had supper with Biddy and Joe in the best parlour[1]. I told Biddy that I would not leave Joe alone, but would come to see him very often. Somehow, she didn't seem to believe me.

Also on this visit, I learned that Orlick was still bothering Biddy, which made me feel very worried.

[1] parlour – sitting-room

And there, my sister was laid quietly in the earth while the larks sang high above it, and the light wind strewed it with beautiful shadows of clouds and trees.

On my twenty-first birthday, Mr Jaggers called me into his office. He gave me five hundred pounds and said that I was to receive an income of the same amount each year from now on.

I asked if I would soon know the name of my benefactor[1]. Mr Jaggers reminded me that I was not to ask. It might be years from now, but the person would get in touch with me directly.

I decided I would secretly help Herbert Pocket, who had no expectations or prospects of his own. I wanted to provide him with a small income, about a hundred pounds a year, and eventually buy him a small partnership in a firm. Mr Wemmick agreed to help me. His friend Miss Skiffins' brother was an accountant; Wemmick promised to ask his advice about what I wanted to do.

Some time later, Herbert came home with the news that he had met a young man from a firm called Clarriker's House. Perhaps this was the opportunity he had been waiting for. It was a very happy day when he became a partner in the firm. I was happy too, because I had been able to help him.

[1] benefactor – a person who gives financial support to another person

I sought advice from Wemmick's experience and knowledge of men and affairs, how I could best try with my resources to help Herbert to some present income – say of a hundred a year.

Miss Havisham wanted Estella to visit her at Satis House for a day. I was to accompany Estella on the coach.

For the first time, Miss Havisham and Estella had a disagreement. Miss Havisham was upset because Estella was cold towards her. She had given Estella everything: a good education, beautiful clothes, jewels. But she had taught Estella not to give her love to anyone. Now she was upset because Estella showed no love for her.

Miss Havisham seemed unable to understand that Estella was what she had made her. She had taught Estella to be proud and hard. Now, she was very unhappy because Estella was proud and hard towards her. Estella could only behave as she had been taught. Miss Havisham became so upset that she tore at her hair, moaning and shrieking, and talking wildly. None of this seemed to affect Estella.

I went for a walk in the garden. When I returned Miss Havisham had calmed down. We ended the evening with Estella and I playing cards as usual. I never again saw another outburst such as the one on that evening.

'So hard, so hard!' moaned Miss Havisham, with her former action.
'Who taught me to be hard?' returned Estella. 'Who praised me when I learned my lesson?'

Herbert and I joined the Finches, a young men's club. Drummle was also a member there, and one day boasted about his friendship with Estella. Drummle and Estella! That was a terrible shock.

I had a worse shock to come, however. One night Herbert was away on business. As I sat reading, I heard a noise on the stairs. Looking down, I saw a rough man with long grey hair. He asked to come in and sat down in a chair by the fire. Suddenly I knew him! It was the convict that I had helped all those years ago.

He told me that he had been transported to Australia for life. He had become a sheep farmer and stock breeder, and made a lot of money. And he … was my benefactor! Not Miss Havisham, but a convict. He had set out to make me a gentleman. It was the thought of helping me that had kept him going. Even now, he was risking his life to see me.

I gave him Herbert's bed for the night and fell asleep in front of the fire. My dreams of Estella and Miss Havisham were just that, dreams. I now had no real connection with them, or with Satis House.

'Look'ee here, Pip. I'm your second father. You're my son – more to me nor any son. I've put away money, only for you to spend.'

Volume Three

I awoke during the night. The candles were burnt out and the fire was dead. I went to find the night watchman to get a light. On the stairs, I fell over a man crouching in the corner. When I returned with the watchman, the man was gone.

Next morning I learned that my convict's name was Abel Magwitch. On his journey back to England he had used the name 'Provis'. We decided to continue with that.

Provis looked like a hungry old dog, and his manners were terrible. He was proud of what he had done for me – my lodgings, my clothes, my good manners. He had a pocket-book[1] stuffed with money.

To my horror, he said he was back to stay. He planned to change his appearance. I knew that nothing would hide the fact that he was a convict. If he was caught again, there would be no mercy.

[1] pocket-book – wallet

Now, in groping my way down the black staircase I fell over
something, and that something was a man crouching in
a corner.

The next day, I bought Provis some new clothes and found a room for him to stay nearby. I then called to see Mr Jaggers. He confirmed that Provis, not Miss Havisham, was my benefactor. He didn't want to know about Provis's return. We both pretended he was still in Australia.

Back at Barnard's Inn, Provis put on his new clothes and we cut his hair short. It was no good. To me, he still looked like an escaped prisoner. He seemed to drag one of his legs, as if he still wore a leg-iron, and cut up his food with a jack-knife.

The more Provis admired me and spoke of how proud he was, the more I hated him. Even though he had done so much for me, I longed to run away, leaving him behind me for ever.

I would sit and look at him, wondering what he had done, and loading him with all the crimes in the Calendar, until the impulse was powerful on me to start up and fly from him.

When Herbert returned, he was very surprised to meet my visitor; especially when Provis first threatened him with a knife and then made him swear on the Holy Bible not to 'split' on him. The next morning, at breakfast, Provis told us his story.

Provis had no family and had been in trouble all his life. He had spent a lot of time in prison. He became involved with a man called Compeyson. Compeyson was a crook and a swindler, but he was clever and always made sure that someone else took the blame for his crimes. Compeyson had a friend called Arthur who was ill and dying. Arthur had terrible visions of a woman with a shroud[1]. He died, screaming about his nightmares.

Compeyson and Provis were arrested for using counterfeit[2] money. Because Compeyson was a 'gentleman', he got only half the prison sentence given to Provis.

Herbert listened very carefully, then completed the story for me, writing on a piece of paper. Arthur was Miss Havisham's brother. Compeyson was the man she loved; the man who broke her heart.

[1] shroud – sheet or loose garment for the dead
[2] counterfeit – fake

Herbert had been writing with his pencil in the cover of a book. He softly pushed the book over to me, as Provis stood smoking with his eyes on the fire, and I read in it: 'Young Havisham's name was Arthur. Compeyson is the man who professed to be Miss Havisham's lover.'

Herbert and I decided that I must somehow get Provis out of the country. If Compeyson was alive and found him, he would report Provis to the police. To get Provis abroad, I would have to go, too. First, I had to see Estella and Miss Havisham.

Again I went to the village and stayed at the Blue Boar. There, I met Bentley Drummle who proudly informed me that he was there to see Estella. He had been invited to dine at Satis House that evening. He went riding and I went to Satis House.

When I arrived, Estella and Miss Havisham were sitting together. I told Miss Havisham that I had learned who my benefactor was, and that my expectations had now changed, though I couldn't explain why. I asked her to finish what I had started in helping Herbert Pocket. It would have to remain our secret; Herbert would never know.

Next, I spoke to Estella about my love for her. But I was too late; she had already made up her mind. She and Drummle were to be married!

Estella was part of me. I felt as though my life was over. In despair I left Satis House and walked all the way back to London.

Drummle glanced at me, with an insolent look of triumph on his great-jowled face that cut me to the heart, dull as he was.

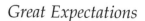

While I was away, Wemmick had found out that 'Provis' was in danger: Compeyson was in London. Wemmick spoke to Herbert, who acted quickly. There was an empty flat at the house where his fiancée, Clara, stayed with her father. It was right on the river. He moved Provis there. Wemmick pointed out that, being on the river already, we could get Provis on to a passenger boat as it left London.

I went immediately. Herbert was there already, and I met Clara for the first time. I could see why he loved her. She was pretty and charming. Provis was very comfortable, though Clara's father, who was not well, made a lot of noise.

Herbert suggested that I fetch my boat from Hammersmith. When we were ready to try to move Provis, we could take him down the river to meet a steamer going abroad. In the meantime, we arranged a signal with Provis: if everything was all right, he would pull down his blind. I rowed on the river often, and the blind was always pulled down.

When Provis first returned I hated him for not being the benefactor I had imagined. Now I found myself starting to care for him. I was glad he was safe.

I was looking at her with pleasure and admiration, when suddenly the growl swelled into a roar again, and a frightful bumping noise was heard above, as if a giant with a wooden leg were trying to bore it through the ceiling to come at us. Upon this Clara said to Herbert, 'Papa wants me, darling!' and ran away.

One night I went to see Mr Wopsle in a pantomime. Afterwards, he told me that, sitting behind me in the audience, he had seen one of the convicts from the marshes long ago. From his description, I knew it must be Compeyson. When I told Herbert, we agreed that we had to be very, very careful.

A week later, Mr Jaggers invited Wemmick and me to dinner. Wemmick gave me a message from Miss Havisham. She wanted to see me about 'the business' I had mentioned on my visit to her. Since the business was helping Herbert, I decided to go the next day.

Jaggers knew all about Drummle marrying Estella. I was very worried when he said that Drummle was the kind of man who could sometimes be violent.

There was something about Molly, his housekeeper. She reminded me of someone, but who? Then I realised. She reminded me of Estella. I felt sure that she was Estella's real mother.

On the way home, Wemmick told me how Molly, Jaggers' serving woman, had been on trial, accused of murder. Jaggers had saved the woman's life. She had a child, Wemmick told me – a girl.

But her hands were Estella's hands, and her eyes were Estella's eyes, and if she had reappeared a hundred times I could have been neither more sure nor less sure that my conviction was the truth.

Miss Havisham had asked to see me again. She was willing to help Herbert. I asked her for nine hundred pounds so that I could finish buying his partnership. She agreed, as long as her name was kept secret. She wrote a note instructing Jaggers to give me the money.

At last, it seemed, she realised the hurt she had caused by teaching Estella to be so cold-hearted. She asked me to forgive her for what she had done to Estella and to me.

I forgave her. I told her that I knew her sad story, and that I understood.

As I was about to leave the house, I went back to make sure she was all right. As I looked into her room, she was standing by the fireplace. Suddenly her dress caught fire! She whirled towards me, all in flames.

Desperately, I pulled off my coat, tore the cloth from the table and tried to smother the blaze. Later, when the doctor came, I found that my hands were badly burned. Miss Havisham was alive but badly injured. When I went to her to say goodbye, she was still asking me to forgive her.

In the moment when I was withdrawing my head to go quietly away, I saw a great flaming light spring up. In the same moment, I saw her running at me, shrieking, with a whirl of fire blazing all about her, and soaring at least as many feet above her head as she was high.

When I returned home, Herbert changed the bandages on my burned hands. As he did so, he told me about a conversation he'd had with Provis. Provis had once been with a woman for four or five years. They had a child together, a little girl.

The woman had been wild and violent. She became jealous of another woman that Provis knew. One day, the other woman was found dead. The mother of Provis's child was tried for murder. It was Jaggers who had defended her and won the case. She was acquitted[1]. Telling Provis that she was going to kill the child, she disappeared. He never saw either of them again. That was why he had been kind to me. I was the same age as his little girl would have been.

Here was the missing piece of the puzzle: I was now sure that Provis was Estella's father.

I went to Jaggers to arrange to get the cheque for Herbert's partnership. I also told him that I now knew who Estella's parents were. Without admitting anything, he suggested that letting out the secrets now would help no one, especially not Estella. The secrets needed to be kept.

---

[1] acquitted – cleared of the crime and released

'I think it would hardly serve her, to establish her parentage for the information of her husband, and to drag her back to disgrace, after an escape of twenty years, pretty secure to last for life.'

Herbert's partnership was paid for at last. His and Clara's future was safe. He would never know where the money came from.

A message from Wemmick told us that we needed to move Provis very soon. With my burned hands, I couldn't row the boat. We decided to ask our old friend, Startop, to help us.

After making arrangements, I returned to Barnard's Inn. There I found a mysterious note telling me to go to a small house on the marshes near the village. My 'Uncle Provis' was mentioned. I went straight away.

When I reached the house, I was attacked from behind. It was a trap, set by Orlick. He had always hated me and now he had me in his power. He tied me to the wall. I almost fainted with the pain in my hands and arms.

I had caused him to lose his job at Satis House. He said that I had come between him and Biddy. And he boasted that he was the one who had attacked my sister. It was obvious that he had been drinking heavily. He was drinking now.

He had been drinking, and his eyes were red and bloodshot. Around his neck was slung a tin bottle, as I had often seen his meat and drink slung about him in other days. He brought the bottle to his lips, and took a fiery drink from it; and I smelt the strong spirits that I saw flash into his face.

Orlick knew all about Provis and Compeyson. He must have been spying on me for weeks. He was the man I had seen on my stairs the night Provis arrived.

He moved to attack me with a stone-hammer and I shouted at the top of my voice. To my amazement the door flew open and three figures rushed in. Orlick leapt over them all and escaped into the night.

It was Herbert and Startop, and Trabb's boy. Herbert had found Orlick's note, which I had dropped on the floor at Barnard's Inn, and, with Startop, had set out to find me. Trabb's boy, by now a young man, had seen me go to the empty house and had guided them there.

Herbert, Startop and I returned to London. My hands were extremely painful after being tied up. I rested for a few hours, then we set off again down the river. It was time for Provis and me to leave the country.

In the same instant I heard responsive shouts, saw figures and a gleam of light dash in at the door, heard voices and tumult, and saw Orlick emerge from a struggle of men, as if it were tumbling water, clear the table at a leap, and fly out into the night.

There were two steamers the next day, the first going to Hamburg, the second to Rotterdam – either would do very well. At first the plan went smoothly. Herbert, Startop and I collected Provis. We spent the night at an inn. There we were told about another boat, a four-oared galley[1], which had been seen earlier. It was thought that the men in the boat were customs officers. This news made us uneasy.

The next day, the first steamer we had planned to meet was almost on top of us when a four-oared galley shot out from the bank. The men on board shouted at us to hand over Provis, who they knew to be Magwitch. They were very close now. Suddenly, Magwitch reached across and pulled the cloak off one of the men in the galley. It was Compeyson! He and Magwitch struggled and they both went overboard. Our boat capsized and we all ended up in the water.

We were all saved except Compeyson. With Magwitch, shackled once more, and weak and ill, we were taken back to the inn. My feelings towards Magwitch had now changed. This man who had the best of intentions for me, was now back in chains. I resolved to be as good a friend to him as he had been to me.

---

[1] four-oared galley – single-decked boat with four oarsmen

Still in the same moment, I saw that the face disclosed, was the face of the other convict of long ago. Still in the same moment, I saw the face tilt backward with a white terror on it that I shall never forget, and heard a great cry on board the steamer and a loud splash in the water, and felt the boat sink from under me.

Magwitch was now in prison awaiting trial. During the next few weeks, there were many changes in my life. Magwitch's pocket-book full of money had been taken by officers when he was arrested. My income had ceased.

Herbert, now a partner in his firm, was sent to Cairo. He planned to come back and marry Clara as soon as possible. Knowing that I would be alone, they asked me to join them in their new life. I needed a little time to think about their kind offer.

Wemmick and Miss Skiffins had a quiet wedding, with his Aged Parent 'giving away' the bride.

Being so ill, Magwitch was moved to the prison hospital, where I was able to visit him every day. A trial was held, and he was sentenced to death. Through it all he behaved with enormous dignity. I stayed at his side and held his hand tightly.

I wrote to the Home Secretary and everyone I could think of, asking for him to be allowed to die in peace. Magwitch grew weaker and weaker. He died before he could be hanged. In his last moments, I told him that his child was alive – and that I loved her. I would always love her.

Rising for a moment, a distinct speck of face in this way of light, the prisoner said, 'My Lord, I have received my sentence of death from the Almighty, but I bow to yours,' and sat down again.

After Magwitch died, I had time to think about my situation. I had many debts. I had been spending far too much money. With all the worry, I became very ill. I had a bad fever, with terrible nightmares. Faces drifted in and out of my confused dreams. Eventually, one face stayed. It was dear Joe, faithful Joe. He had received word that I was ill and had come immediately. He stayed with me and nursed me back to health.

As I recovered, we spoke about many things. There was news of the village. Miss Havisham had died. Orlick had been in trouble again and was in jail. I found myself remembering Biddy and what a fine person she was. I thought of marrying her and almost shared these thoughts with Joe, but didn't. When I was well again, Joe slipped quietly back to the village. He had paid all my bills.

I returned to the village to ask Biddy to be my wife. But first, I went to Satis House. It was being sold.

I arrived at the forge to find Joe and Biddy celebrating their marriage. Seeing their happiness, I was very glad that I hadn't told Joe of my feelings for Biddy.

I looked at both of them, from one to the other, and then—
'It's my wedding-day,' cried Biddy, in a burst of happiness,
'and I am married to Joe!'

There was nothing now to keep me in England.
I went to join Herbert and Clara abroad. Herbert and
I both did well with his firm. We were not rich, but
we lived comfortably. At last, Clarriker told Herbert
who had paid for his partnership. My secret was out.

It was eleven years before I returned again to the
village. Biddy and Joe were very happy and had a
little son named Pip.

I went to see the place where Satis House had been.
There, in what remained of the garden, I met –
Estella! She was as beautiful as ever, but somehow
different. We were warm and comfortable together
and spoke quietly about our separate lives. Estella
had had some very unhappy years. I gathered that
she was no longer married to Drummle.

Holding hands, we walked out of the garden.
Although we said goodbye, I somehow felt that
we would not be parted again.

I took her hand in mine, and we went out of the ruined place; and, as the morning mists had risen long ago when I first left the forge, so, the evening mists were rising now, and in all the broad expanse of tranquil light they showed to me, I saw the shadow of no parting from her.

Also available in the
Graphic Novels Series:

THE MAYOR OF CASTERBRIDGE
THOMAS HARDY

Retold by Hilary Burningham

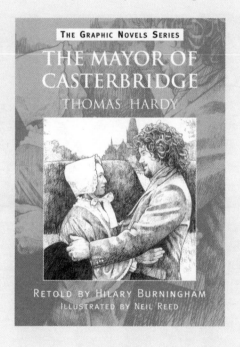

See over for details of our Graphic Shakespeare Series

*If you enjoyed reading this book,
you may wish to read other books in the
sister series:*

The Graphic Shakespeare Series

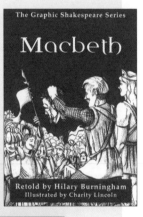

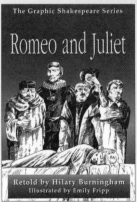

The titles in the Graphic Shakespeare Series
are an ideal introduction to Shakespeare's
plays, but can equally well be used
as revision aids.

The main characters and key events
are brought to life in the simplified story
and dramatic pictures, and the short extracts
from the original play focus on key speeches
in Shakespeare's language.

*Available in the
Graphic Shakespeare Series:*

**A Midsummer Night's Dream
Henry V
Julius Caesar
Macbeth
Richard III
Romeo and Juliet
The Tempest
Twelfth Night
Much Ado About Nothing**

EVANS BROTHERS LIMITED